The Berenstain Bears®
STORIES TO SHARE WITH
MAMA BEAR

Includes:

The Berenstain Bears and   MAMA'S NEW JOB

When Mama gets home
Too late for a meal,
How will the cubs
And Papa Bear feel?

The Berenstain Bears and the BAD HABIT

The Berenstain Bears and the MAMA'S DAY SURPRISE

STAN & JAN BERENSTAIN

Random House 🏠 New York

Copyright © 1984, 1986, 2004, 2021 by Berenstain Enterprises, Inc.
All rights reserved.
Published in the United States by Random House Children's Books, a division of
Penguin Random House LLC, 1745 Broadway, New York, NY 10019, and in Canada by
Penguin Random House Canada Limited, Toronto. Originally published in different form by
Random House Children's Books, New York, as *The Berenstain Bears and Mama's New Job*
in 1984, *The Berenstain Bears and the Bad Habit* in 1986, and *The Berenstain Bears and
the Mama's Day Surprise* in 2004.

Random House and the colophon are registered trademarks of Penguin Random House LLC.

Visit us on the Web!
rhcbooks.com
BerenstainBears.com

Library of Congress Control Number: 2020934605
ISBN 978-0-593-18222-2 (hardcover)

MANUFACTURED IN CHINA
10 9 8 7 6 5 4 3 2 1

The Berenstain Bears
and MAMA'S NEW JOB

Supper will be a little late — Love, Mama

When Mama gets home
Too late for a meal,
How will the cubs
And Papa Bear feel?

The Bear family, who lived in the big tree house down a sunny dirt road deep in Bear Country, was a very happy family. One of the reasons was that they were all very *busy*. Each member of the family had work to do. Papa Bear cut and split logs and made the wood into handsome furniture which he was proud to sell.

Mama Bear not only took care of her family, but she managed the whole tree house and tended the vegetable patch as well.

And, of course, Brother and Sister Bear had important jobs too: going to school and keeping up with their schoolwork.

The members of the Bear family had hobbies, too. Papa's favorite hobbies were fishing and napping. He caught almost as many naps as he caught fish. Brother and Sister also had many hobbies. Brother was especially proud of his model airplanes. He liked to have Mama watch him fly his models, and sometimes she helped him fly his tether plane.

Sister was a super rope-jumper and her goal was to jump a thousand times without a miss. She liked to have Mama count for her because Sister could jump faster than she could count.

Since Mama was so busy with her household duties, she had time for just one hobby— but what a hobby! Mama was the best quilt maker in all of Bear Country! Her quilts were light and fluffy, but very warm. Her stitchery was fine and even. And her designs were original and exciting.

Sister Bear slept cozy and warm under a quilt that showed her jumping rope. Brother went to sleep under a handsome airplane design. And the big quilt on Mama and Papa's bed showed the Bear family's beautiful tree house.

HOME SWEET TREE

Yes, the members of the Bear family had happy, busy, full lives. Especially Mama.

"My dear," called Papa to Mama as she worked in the vegetable patch, "if it wouldn't be too much trouble, would you put aside any fishing worms you might find?"

"Look, Mama!" called Brother. "I'm going to fly my new biplane!"

"I'm going to try for a thousand, Mama!" said Sister. "Would you please count for me?"

A little *too* full, thought Mama from time to time. She would have liked to have a little more time for her quilts. She had some lovely design ideas she wanted to try:

a sunburst with clouds and bluebirds...

14

a beautiful bouquet of
flowers with butterflies...

and a harvest scene
with pumpkins and
squash.

But there just never seemed
to be enough time.

15

Then one day something happened that changed the lives of the Bear family—

something that changed Mama's
quilt-making from a hobby . . .

. . . into a business!

It might not have happened except for a coincidence, which is when two things happen at the same time.

The two things that happened were that Papa had a big sale of some very special furniture, and on the same day Mama hung out the family quilts to air.

Folks who came to buy Papa's handsome furniture became excited about Mama's beautiful quilts and wanted to buy them, too. Would-be buyers offered Mama quite a lot of money. They were very disappointed when she told them that the quilts were not for sale.

"With your talent, you really should be in business!" they said.

"Mama in business?" said Papa, patting her on the shoulder. "I don't think so. One business-bear in the family is enough."

But Mama wasn't so sure. She was proud of her quilt-making skills and knowledge. After all, she *was* president of the Bear Country Quilting Club. Other quilt makers often came to her for help and advice.

That evening Papa and the cubs noticed that Mama was very quiet.

She was quiet during supper.

She was quiet during cleanup.

She was quiet all evening. She was quiet because she was thinking—thinking about going into business.

The next day at lunch she made her big announcement.

"I've decided to open up a quilt shop," she said, "and I've rented the empty store just down the road."

"Not that overgrown wreck that's been empty for years!" protested Papa.

"But you don't want to be a business-bear," said Sister. "You're our mama!"

"That's no reason why I shouldn't open my own quilt shop. A lot of mama bears have jobs: Mrs. Grizzle is a sitter; Mrs. Honeybear teaches school; Dr. Gert Grizzly is your pediatrician. . . ."

"Yeah," said Brother, "but they're not our mama!"
"There's really nothing to worry about," said Mama.
"Things aren't going to be all that different."

"Will you still count for me when I jump rope?" asked Sister.

"And will you still watch me fly my airplanes?" Brother wanted to know.

"And how about my fishing worms?" asked Papa. "Will you still put them aside for me when you tend to the vegetable patch?"

"We'll see about all that," Mama said. "Meanwhile, I have to be at the shop. Some of my quilt club friends are helping me get it ready—and, oh yes," she added as she turned to leave, "there's a lot to do, so supper may be a little late tonight. Ta-ta!"

"Ta-ta," said Papa.
"Ta-ta," said the cubs.

Supper wasn't a little late that night. It was a lot late—and it was Papa and the cubs who prepared it. But they didn't mind, because although Mama was very tired, she was very happy, too—happy and excited!

"Guess what!" said Sister as she served Mama her supper. "I reached a thousand jumps today! Brother counted for me!"

"And Sis helped me fly my tether plane! We had a great flight!" added Brother.

"And I weeded the vegetable patch," said Papa, bringing a tub of warm water to Mama for her tired feet.

"Well," said Mama. "I'm very proud of you all."

Papa and the cubs were very proud of her, too. There was no way to tell whether the quilt shop would be a success, but she certainly was giving it a good try.

After about two weeks of hard work, the Bear Country Quilt Shop had its grand opening. It was a very exciting event! Not only did Mama sell her own quilts, but she sold quilts for all the members of her club as well.

It was a great success. Why, even Mayor and Mrs. Honeypot came in their long lavender limousine. They bought one quilt and ordered three more!

"I know what!" said Mama as she closed up shop that night. "Let's stop off at the Burger Bear for supper! My treat!"

The Bear family celebrated with a delicious Burger Bear supper. Papa and the cubs were very proud of their business-bear wife and mama.

The extra money came in handy too!

The Berenstain Bears

and the

BAD HABIT

Habits & tics —

When cubs start to twitch
or to scratch or to nibble,
what they need is some help,
not a lecture or quibble.

Cub Care

Sister Bear, who lived with her mama, papa, and brother in the big tree house down a sunny dirt road deep in Bear Country, had been going to school for quite a while.

First there had been nursery school, which was pure fun—playing with dolls and blocks, rolling clay snakes, and scribbling with crayons.

Next had come kindergarten. That was fun too. There were marching games and rhythm band. She also learned a lot of numbers in kindergarten—and most of the alphabet.

Now Sister was in first grade. Regular school was different. It was still fun and she liked Teacher Jane very much, but it wasn't *all* fun. There was quite a lot of work—spelling, number problems, all kinds of things.

In regular school you have to concentrate—
and sometimes when you concentrate, you form
little nervous habits. That's what happened
to some of the cubs in Teacher Jane's class.

Lizzy twirled her fur.
Twirl, twirl, twirl.

Freddy scratched his head.
Scratch, scratch, scratch.

Norman sucked his thumb.
Suck, suck, suck.

And Sister nibbled her nails.
Nibble, nibble, nibble, nibble.

Before she knew it, she had nibbled them down to nubbins. In fact, she nibbled them down so far that some of her fingers were getting sore.

40

"Oh, dear!" said Mama Bear to
Sister when the cubs got home
from school one day. "You've
nibbled your nails down to
nubbins. In fact, you've nibbled
them clean off. How did it happen?"

"I'm not exactly sure, Mama,"
Sister said. "But some of them
are getting sore."

"Hmm," said Mama. "Well, here's what we'll do. We'll put a little medicine on the sore ones and bits of adhesive tape on all of them. That will remind you not to nibble and will give them a chance to grow back."

42

The bits of tape helped Sister remember not to nibble, but they also got in the way when she tried to do certain things. It's very hard to hold a pencil with tape all over your fingertips,

or change the channel,

or scratch when you have an itch.

And when Sister tried to play jacks, she couldn't get any higher than twosies.

43

But worst of all, the bits
of tape told the whole world
that Sister Bear was a nail biter.

The next morning, when Sister lined up for school, Lizzy Bruin and some others began pointing and teasing. "Sister nibbles her nails! Sister nibbles her nails!" It didn't take Sister long to decide to pull off those bits of tape!

And without the tape, she forgot to remember not to nibble.

She forgot during school.

She forgot on the bus.

She even forgot as she and Brother climbed off the bus.

"You're going to have to cut that out, Sis," said Brother, "or you'll get to be a regular full-time nail biter."

48

"I'm afraid your brother's right," said Mama, who was organizing the wheelbarrow for some garden work. "I don't mean to nag, but nail biting is a very difficult habit to break."

"Habit?" asked Sister, making fists so that her nubby, nibbled-off nails wouldn't show. "What's a habit?"

49

"That's a good question," said Mama. "Come along while I plant these tulip bulbs Grizzly Gran sent over and we'll talk about it.

"A habit," Mama said as she pushed the wheelbarrow along the well-worn path, "is something you do so often you don't even have to think about it. Habits are a very important part of our lives. And most of them are good—like brushing your teeth and combing your fur when you get up in the morning, and looking both ways before you cross a road. But some habits aren't so good."

"Like nail biting?" asked Sister.

"You *would* like to have your nice nails grow back, wouldn't you?" was Mama's answer.

"Oh, yes!" said Sister. "But I keep forgetting! Why is it so hard to remember?"

"Well," said Mama, "it's sort of like this path. I've wheeled this barrow over it so many times that it's worn a deep rut right down the middle. And it keeps getting deeper every time I use it. Why, it's so deep now that I can't get out of it without a little help.

"That's the way it is with a bad habit—the more you use it, the harder it is to get out of it. Here, this is where I want to plant the bulbs."

"What about my nail-biting habit?" asked Sister as she helped Mama out of the deep rut. "How am I going to get out of it?"

"You just need a little help, that's all," said Mama. "Let's plant Gran's tulips while I think about it. And later I'll talk to your papa. He may have some ideas."

54

"I could read the riot act to her," suggested Papa. "You know: 'Nail biting is an outrageous, disgraceful habit and if you don't stop it immediately—'"

"Dear me, no!" said Mama. "Nail biting is a kind of nervous habit, and shouting and threatening will just make her more nervous."

"I suppose so," said Papa thoughtfully. "Perhaps some sort of reward would help. A bit of money—let's say a dime for every day she doesn't bite her nails."

Before Mama could answer, Sister Bear, who had been nervously nibbling in the next room, popped in and said, "A dime—ten whole cents every day just for not biting my nails?"

"That's right," said Papa. "Until the habit's broken."

"I'll never nibble again!" she said as she thought of all those lovely dimes she was going to get.

But the way it turned out, she didn't get a single dime. All she got was discouraged.

A day is a long time and habits are powerful—especially bad habits. Even with the promise of a dime, Sister couldn't remember not to nibble. Mama and Papa got discouraged too.

"Oh, well," sighed Mama. "Life goes on. I must call Gran and thank her for the tulip bulbs."

"Oh, you're very welcome, my dear," said Gran when Mama called. "And how is everything at your house?...Is that so?... You know, I was a nail biter when I was a cub and my mama helped me to stop. What have you tried so far?...Um...Uh-huh... Well, I think you're on the right track with the dime, but instead of a dime, and instead of giving it to her at the *end* of the day..."

"What an interesting idea," said Mama as she listened to wise old Grizzly Gran.

So they tried Gran's idea. Instead of a dime at the *end* of each day, they gave Sister ten pennies—one for each nail—at the *beginning* of each day. Ten pennies to keep—*unless she nibbled.*

And with those pennies in her pocket,

jiggling when she got on the school bus,

jingling when she jumped rope in the schoolyard...

...just waiting to be remembered when some nail decided it needed a nibble...

the plan worked!

Not perfectly. It's hard to break a habit, and Sister had to give back some of those pennies. But in ten days she had ninety-three pennies!

And even better: she had
ten fine fingernails.

Great for picking things up,

changing the channel,

and scratching itches.

And the next time she played jacks, she got all the way to tensies!

"Phew!" said Papa Bear. "I'm glad that's over."

"Yes, indeed!" agreed Mama, breathing a great sigh of relief.

That's when Brother Bear looked at his fingernails and piped up, "You know, I think I might start biting my nails—I could use the money."

"I certainly hope you're joking!"
roared Papa. "Because if you're not—"
"I'm joking. I'm joking," interrupted
Brother.

And he was—sort of.

The Berenstain Bears
and the
MAMA'S DAY SURPRISE

Some mama bears are
so all-seeing and wise,
when Mother's Day comes
they're hard to surprise.

Mother's Day was coming, and Mama Bear knew that Papa and the cubs were going to surprise her with a special celebration.

Last year they took her out for a special Mother's Day dinner.

Mama was pretty sure that this year they were going to surprise her with a special Mother's Day breakfast in bed. And alas, she also knew that she would probably have to spend the rest of Mother's Day cleaning up the mess they made preparing her special breakfast in bed. But that was okay. It's the thought that counts.

The signs of Papa and the cubs' Mother's Day plan weren't hard to read.

There was a marker in the cookbook at the page for Mama's favorite breakfast: honeyed French toast with blueberries.

And one day when they were shopping at
the Beartown Mart, she saw the cubs slip off
in the direction of the card department.

As Mother's Day drew closer, Mama knew
that she had a lot to do if her family's Mother's
Day surprise was going to be a success.

First, she had to find the old bed tray they used when a family member was ill. She found it at the top of one of the kitchen cabinets where she kept jars and bottles that were too nice to throw away. It had some oatmeal on it from when Papa had been in bed with a cold. She scraped off the oatmeal and put the bed tray where she knew Papa and the cubs could find it.

But there was more to do. She had to make sure they would have the ingredients to make her special Mother's Day surprise. She checked the recipe in the cookbook. Honeyed French toast with blueberries called for honey, bread, eggs, sweet cream, sweet butter, powdered sugar, and blueberries. It was Papa and the cubs' favorite breakfast, too. But that was okay. It's the thought that counts. As for the mess they would make in the kitchen—well, that just came with being a mama.

Mama checked the cupboard. There was honey, of course, and plenty of bread.

There was powdered sugar, too. But it was all caked up like a rock.

They were out of eggs. But that wouldn't be a problem. She could get farm-fresh eggs from Farmer Ben. Nor would sweet cream, sweet butter, and powdered sugar be a problem. She would get those at the supermarket. But fresh blueberries? It was much too early in the season for blueberries.

The cubs were with Mama on her next trip to the supermarket. She didn't want to spoil their surprise, so she gave them a little shopping list to take care of while she put sweet cream, sweet butter, and powdered sugar into her cart.

She also bought some extra cleanser and scouring pads for the big Mother's Day cleanup.

She looked high and low for blueberries, but there were none to be found. It turned out that Gran had frozen some last season. That took care of the blueberries.

Mama was also pretty sure that a new bathrobe was going to be part of her Mother's Day surprise. She caught the cubs checking the size of her old threadbare one. But she pretended not to notice. As the big day drew closer, Mama made sure to stay out of the way when she thought they might be wrapping presents.

Finally it was the night before the morning of the big surprise. Papa and the cubs were doing their best not to let on that anything the least bit special was happening. But their secret smiles gave them away.

"Now, here's the plan," said Papa while Mama was off putting baby Honey Bear to bed. "I'm setting my wristwatch alarm for five o'clock in the morning. I'll set the alarm low so it won't wake Mama.

"Then I'll slip out of bed and come wake you two, and we'll sneak downstairs to the kitchen. Now, it's going to be very dark, so we'll have to be careful not to bump into things or we'll wake Mama."

Mama pretended to be asleep when Papa's alarm went off. She lay perfectly still as Papa slipped out of bed.

There was a certain amount of bumping and thumping as Papa and the cubs stumbled around in the dark. Papa even slipped and almost fell down the stairs, but the cubs caught him.

Mama lay awake getting ready to be surprised. But it wasn't easy. From the sound of it, things didn't seem to be going well down in the kitchen. The sound of an eggbeater was to be expected. But then there was a big clunk. What happened? Oh, dear. It wouldn't be the first time Papa dropped the bowl while he was beating eggs.

And what was that burnt smell? They must have burnt the toast.

Mama could just picture the mess they were making in the kitchen. It was all she could do to stay in bed. But after a few more clunks and some muffled shouts, she slipped out of bed, put on her old bathrobe, and stole downstairs to sneak a look at the kitchen.

It was the worst kitchen mess she had ever seen. The bowl had broken, so there was broken crockery and egg all over the floor. There was burnt toast on the drainboard and a sticky honey handprint on the wall.

Oh, dear, thought Mama, it's going to take me a week to clean up the mess. Thank goodness Mother's Day comes just once a year.

But out of the wreckage of broken crockery, spilled eggs, burnt toast, and sticky honey, Papa and the cubs had managed to put together a beautiful breakfast tray of Mama's favorites:

Honeyed French toast with blueberries, sassafras tea, and even a small vase of red roses.

Mama sighed. It was so beautiful that it was almost worth the terrible mess they had made.

But now they were coming
out of the kitchen and heading
for the stairs. Mama had to
get out of there or the whole
surprise would be ruined.
She scurried up the stairs
and climbed back into bed.

She pretended to be just waking up when they came into the room with her breakfast tray.

"Happy Mother's Day!" said Brother and Sister.

"Happy Mother's Day, my dear," said Papa as he placed the tray on the bed and plumped the pillow behind Mama's back.

"Mother's Day?" said Mama. "Well, I suppose it is! How lovely! All my favorites: honeyed French toast with blueberries and sassafras tea and these beautiful roses. And look! Just what I needed!" she said as she unwrapped the new bathrobe.

"This is absolutely delicious!" said Mama as she ate her French toast and sipped her sassafras tea. "I don't know how to thank you."

Just then they heard baby Honey Bear's cry of *"Mama! Mama!"*

"I'd better get Honey Bear up and give her breakfast," said Mama.

"No," said Papa. "This is Mother's Day. You just stay in bed and read your cards. The cubs and I will take care of everything."

And they did.

When Mama got downstairs to go to work on the kitchen, she got a *real* surprise. It was the cleanest, shiniest, spick-and-spannest kitchen she had ever seen.

"Well," said Sister, "how did you like your Mama's Day surprise?"

"Yes," said Brother. "How did you like it?" Honey Bear gurgled and Papa beamed.

"How did I like it?" she said. "It was the most wonderful surprise any mama ever had!"

Then she gave her cubs
a great big Mama Bear hug.